Please return or renew this item before the latest date shown below

Renewals can be made
by internet   www.onfife.com/fife-libraries
in person   at any library in Fife
by phone   03451 55 00 66

ON
AT FIFE
LIBRARIES

Thank you for using your library

Thank you for using your library

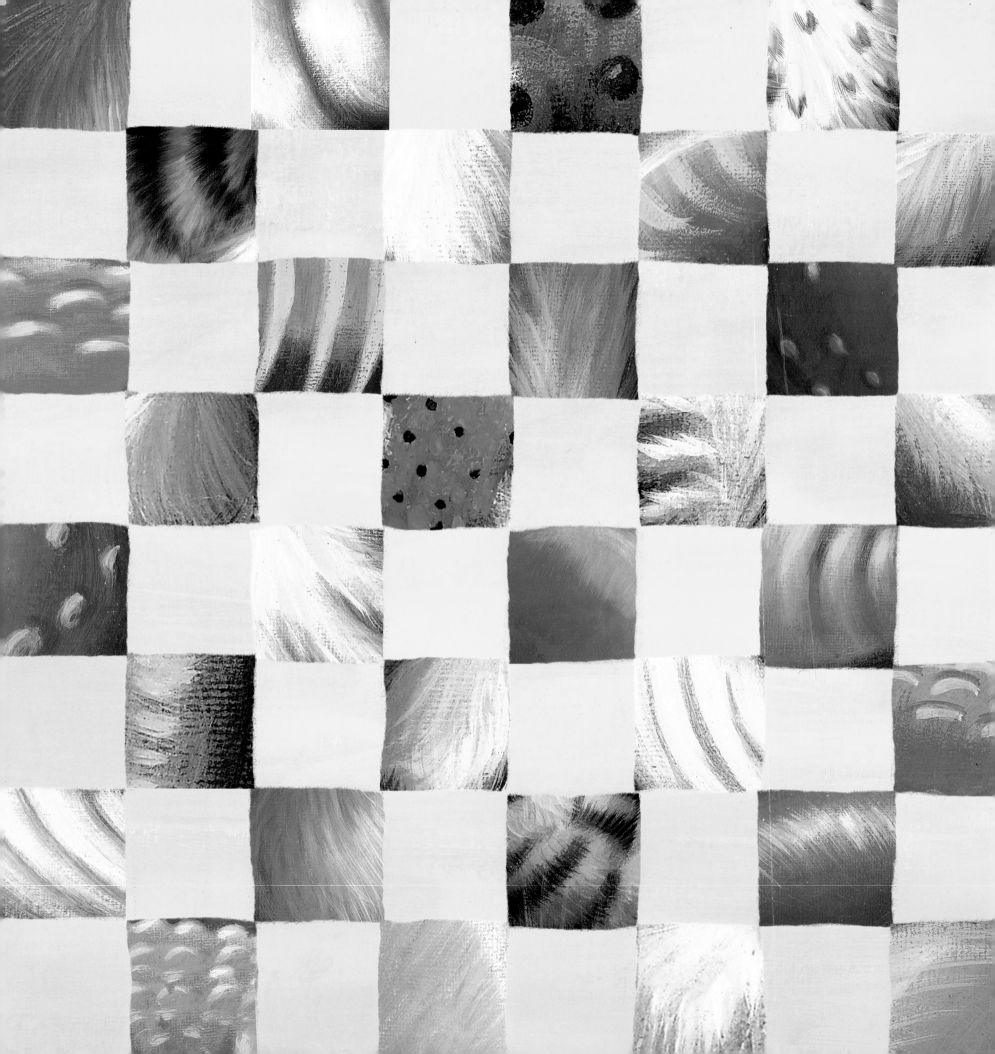

For my daddy
J.H.

For my dad x
R.E.

First published 2013 by Macmillan Children's Books
a division of Macmillan Publishers Limited
20 New Wharf Road, London N1 9RR
Basingstoke and Oxford
Associated companies throughout the world
www.panmacmillan.com

ISBN: 978-0-230-76685-3 (HB)
ISBN: 978-1-4472-1972-9 (PB)

Text copyright © Julia Hubery 2013
Illustrations copyright © Rebecca Elliott 2013
Moral rights asserted.

2 4 6 8 9 7 5 3 1

A CIP catalogue record for this book is available from the British Library.

Printed in China

My Daddy

Written by
Julia Hubery

Illustrated by
Rebecca Elliott

MACMILLAN CHILDREN'S BOOKS

Dads are so different all over the world,
with feathers or fins, or tails that are curled.

Some dads are big and some dads are small,
but whose dad is really the best of them all?

"My kangaroo dad
can bounce anywhere.
He stamps his big feet
and zooms through the air.

I jump on his back,

and we aim for the sky . . .

then take off so fast, it's as if we can fly!"

ROAR!

"Everyone shakes when
my tiger dad roars!
He shows off his teeth
and stretches his claws.

When animals see him, they tremble and fuss . . .

but when he's with me, he's a big softie-puss!"

"Beware of Dad's teeth when it's time for a snack,
and watch his strong tail – it can splish, splash and WHACK!

I always feel safe with my dad at my side,
but it's even more fun when he gives me a ride!"

"My dad is a supermouse, BIG, BRAVE and STRONG!

He comes to my rescue
if something goes wrong.

He sneaks out for food so the cat never sees . . .

then we picnic all day on our favourite cheese!"

"My dad's great at hiding
and so hard to spot,

at times I don't know
if I see him or not.

He changes so quickly to match any scene . . .

but in no time at all, he's back to bright green!"

"When I creep up on Dad for a sneaky surprise,
he catches me out with his magical eyes!

We stay up all night
until early birds sing . . .

then I sleep all day long, tucked under Dad's wing. "

"Nobody's daddy has long legs like these,
they bend, curl and stick to whatever we please.

You'd think all our legs might get us in muddles,
but they're the best way to give big octocuddles!"

"Dad's brilliant at swinging, he'd win any race . . .

and get the first prize
for the funniest face!

"When the sun starts to set, I close my tired eyes, and rock in Dad's tail as he sings lullabies."

"Who needs a tail
	with my dad's nifty nose?
It can throw me and catch me,
	and tickle my toes.

Squelching in mud
is the best way to play . . .

then Dad sprays me clean at the end of the day!"

"My dad is so big, he's the king of the sea!
We love to go diving, just Daddy and me.

We swim down so deep, then back up we dash
and race to the top where we make a huge SPLASH!"

So whose dad is best
    and what makes him top?
A long, curly nose,
    or a huge, bouncy hop?

However dads look,
   whatever they do,
YOUR dad is the best,
   and he thinks you're great too!

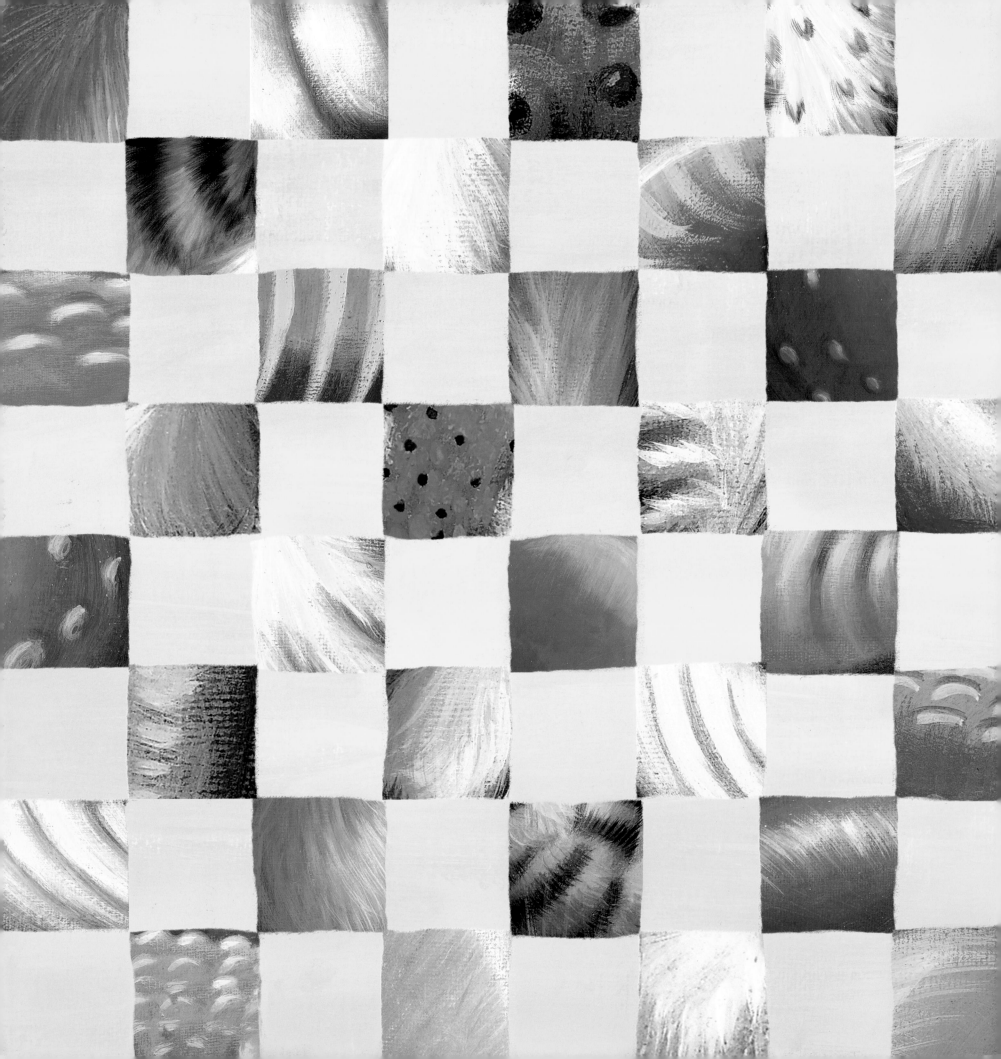